Contents

The Three Billy Goats Gruff.......................6 – 9
(*a traditional folk tale*)

Puss in Boots ....10 – 13
(*based on a story by Charles Perrault*)

The Three Little Pigs..............................14 – 17
(*a traditional folk tale*)

Hansel and Gretel.....................................18 – 21
(*based on a story by Jacob and Wilhelm Grimm*)

The Gingerbread Boy ....22 – 25
(*a traditional folk tale*)

Little Red Riding Hood ....26 – 29
(*based on a story by Charles Perrault*)

Jack and the Beanstalk ....30 – 33
(*a traditional folk tale*)

Goldilocks and the Three Bears...............34 – 37
(*a traditional folk tale*)

The Ugly Duckling...................................38 – 41
(*based on a story by Hans Christian Andersen*)

The Elves and the Shoemaker ....42 – 45
(*based on a story by Jacob and Wilhelm Grimm*)

Material in this edition was previously published by Ladybird Books in *Stories for Bedtime.*

Published by Ladybird Books Ltd
A Penguin Company
Penguin Books Ltd, 80 Strand London WC2R 0RL, UK
Penguin Books Australia Ltd, Camberwell, Victoria, Australia
Penguin Books (NZ) Ltd, Private Bag 102902, NSMC, Auckland, New Zealand

10 9 8 7 6 5

© LADYBIRD BOOKS LTD 1994

Printed in Italy

Ladybird

NURSERY TALES

Retold by BRIAN MORSE
Illustrated by PETER STEVENSON

The Three Billy Goats Gruff

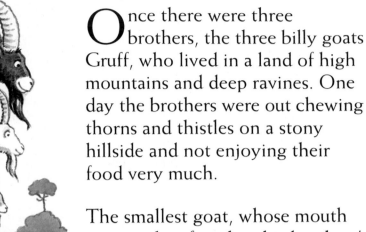

Once there were three brothers, the three billy goats Gruff, who lived in a land of high mountains and deep ravines. One day the brothers were out chewing thorns and thistles on a stony hillside and not enjoying their food very much.

The smallest goat, whose mouth was much softer than his brothers', stopped for a rest. He looked over to the hillside opposite and what did he see? The most luscious green grass a billy goat had ever set eyes on!

"Brothers!" he bleated. "Follow me!" Down the bank he bounded. There was a stream at the bottom with a bridge over it, and the youngest billy goat began to run across the bridge.

"Stop!" his brothers shouted, but far too late. In the ravine under the bridge lived a troll with the sharpest teeth and ugliest eyes in the whole wide world.

"Stop! Stop!" the brothers called, but the troll was already poking his head over the edge of the bridge.

"Who's that trip-trapping over my bridge?" the troll screamed.

When he saw the troll, the smallest billy goat trembled from the tip of his wet nose to the end of his feathery tail.

"I'm little billy goat Gruff," he bleated. "I'm only crossing your bridge to get to the young green grass on the other side."

The troll licked his lips with his enormous rough tongue. "Oh no, you're not!" he shouted. He began to wriggle his way up onto the bridge. "I'm going to gobble you up."

"But my brother's coming after me!" the little billy goat bleated. "And he's much *much* fatter than me."

The greedy troll immediately dropped out of sight and the smallest billy goat ran on over the bridge to the other side.

The two older brothers put their heads together to decide what to do, and a minute later the middle-sized billy goat Gruff rather reluctantly came down the hillside. *Trip, trap, trip, trap,* went his hooves on the bridge. Immediately the troll raised his head above the edge.

"Who's that trip-trapping over my bridge?" he screamed.

7

"I'm middle-sized billy goat Gruff," the goat bleated, "and I'm going across to join my younger brother."

"Oh no, you're not!" the troll shouted. He began to clamber onto the bridge. "You look fat and juicy. I'm going to gobble you up."

"But my other brother's coming after me!" bleated the middle-sized goat, at the same time trying to make himself look as small as possible. "He's much, much, *much* fatter than me."

The greedy troll immediately dropped out of sight and, with a sigh of relief, the middle-sized billy goat ran over to the other side of the bridge.

After a minute the largest billy goat Gruff started trip-trapping over the bridge too. *Trip, trap, trip, trap, trip, trap,* went his hooves on the bridge.

The troll could hardly contain his excitement at the meal he was going to have. "Who's that trip-trapping over my bridge?" he screamed.

"I'm big billy goat Gruff," the third brother bleated, "and I'm going across to the other side to join my brothers in the lovely green grass."

"Oh no, you're not!" the troll shouted. "No, no, no!" With his long hairy arms he pulled himself straight up onto the bridge. "I'm going to gobble you up! That's what's going to happen!"

The moment the troll's feet landed on the bridge, he realized he'd made a big mistake. Big billy goat Gruff was massive. His horns were longer and sharper than all the troll's teeth put together.

As the goat put his head down and charged, the troll screamed, "No, no, no!" He tried to dive back under the bridge, but far too late. The goat's horns tossed him into the stream and the raging water carried him away. No one ever found out what happened to him and no one cared!

The big billy goat Gruff trip-trapped proudly over the rest of the bridge and joined his two brothers. Perhaps he had a few words to say to the smallest billy goat for putting them all in danger, but certainly the Gruffs enjoyed the young green grass and lived happily ever after.

Puss in Boots

Once there was a miller who had three sons. When he died, he left his mill to the eldest son and his donkey to the second son. The youngest got Puss. This made him most unhappy.

"What can you do with a cat?" he protested. "Cats don't even make a decent stew." Puss overheard that and spoke up quickly. "You'll find you haven't got such a bad bargain, Master. Just give me a bag and a pair of boots and you'll see what I can do for you."

Surprised, the boy did as the cat asked. Puss pulled on the boots and admired himself in the mirror. Then he took a lettuce and a juicy carrot from the pantry and marched off into the woods. There he opened the bag, arranged the lettuce and carrot inside, and hid nearby. Soon a tender young rabbit came along. He smelt the tasty vegetables and hopped inside the bag. In a second, Puss leapt up and tied the bag up tight.

Instead of taking the rabbit to his master, however, Puss headed for the palace, where he asked to see the King. Bowing low he said, "Your Majesty, I bring a present from my master, the Marquis." The King was delighted.

For three months Puss brought so many presents to the palace that the King began to look forward to seeing him. Then at last the day Puss had been waiting for arrived. "Don't ask any questions, Master," he said, "but go and bathe in the river this morning." Puss knew that the King would be driving nearby with the Princess, his daughter.

Later that morning, as the King's carriage drew near the river, Puss came rushing up all a-tremble. "Help! Help!" he gasped. "The Marquis, my master, is drowning!" Immediately the King sent a regiment of soldiers to the rescue.

But Puss had not finished. He told the King that while his master had been swimming, robbers had stolen his clothes. (In fact, Puss had hidden his master's rags in some bushes himself!) The King lost no time in sending for a suit of clothes for the Marquis. As you can imagine, Puss's master was feeling very bewildered at his sudden change of name, but he was clever enough to keep quiet.

As soon as the Marquis was decently dressed, the King invited him to ride in his carriage and meet his daughter. The Princess took one look at the Marquis, now dressed up to the nines, and fell in love with him.

Meanwhile Puss ran ahead. Soon he came to a field where some men were mowing grass. "Listen!" he cried. "The King is driving this way. When he asks you whose fields these are, you tell him they belong to my master, the Marquis. If you don't, I'll have you chopped into little pieces!"

Then Puss ran on a little further and came to a field where some men were cutting wheat. He repeated his instructions. Then on he ran again, and whenever he met anyone, he told them the same thing. At last he came to the Ogre's castle.

Slowly the King's carriage followed in Puss's tracks. Each time he came to a group of workers, the King asked them, "Whose are these fields, my good men?" Of course, he always got the same answer! The King was amazed at how much land the Marquis owned. (And so was Puss's master!)

Meanwhile Puss was very busy at the castle. "Ogre," he said, hiding a shudder at the Ogre's bad breath, "I've heard that you have the most amazing magical powers."

"Well, yes," said the Ogre modestly.

"For instance," Puss went on, "I've heard you can change yourself into a lion." In a flash the Ogre changed himself, and Puss fled to the top of a wardrobe, out of harm's way. When the Ogre had returned to normal, Puss came down. "Brilliant!" he said. "But changing into something small, like a mouse, must be impossible for a big fellow like you!"

"Impossible?" laughed the Ogre. "I can do anything!" In a flash he changed into a mouse. And… Puss ate him.

Seconds later the King arrived at the Ogre's castle. You can guess who owned the castle now! Puss met the carriage at the castle gates. "Come this way," he said. "A feast awaits you." (The Ogre had been going to invite a few friends round!)

By the end of the day, Puss's master, the Marquis, was engaged to the Princess. And by the end of the week, they were married. And Puss? Well, he lived to a ripe old age, using up every one of his nine lives, and he never needed to hunt a mouse again—but sometimes he did, just for the sheer fun of it!

13

The Three Little Pigs

Once three little pigs decided it was about time they left home and found their own place to live. No sooner said than done. That very morning they packed up their things, kissed their mother goodbye, and set off.

They walked till midday. Then they sat by the road and ate half their sandwiches. After a nap they set off again. By suppertime the first little pig felt too tired to go any further.

"But we haven't got anywhere yet!" his brother and sister said. "What are you going to do for a house?"

They were next to a field full of wheat that had just been cut. "I'll build a house out of straw," the little pig said. He closed his eyes and went straight to sleep.

When the first little pig woke, the sun was sinking fast and the air was growing cold. And what was that dark hairy shadow in the wood? Suddenly he wished he'd gone on with the others. But he set to work, gathered together some straw, and built his house.

At midnight there came a tapping at his door. "Little pig, little pig, let me come in," a voice said. The little pig's blood ran cold. Now he knew what the shadow had been – a wolf!

"You're not coming in here, not by the hair on my chinny-chin-chin," he said in his most grown-up voice.

"Then I'll huff and I'll puff and I'll blow your house in!" the wolf snarled. "And that'll be the end of you." And it was.

Next morning the other pigs came back. What did they find? A heap of straw and all their brother's belongings torn up and scattered across the field. They ran away as quickly as they could.

By midday the two little pigs were exhausted and stopped running. The second little pig began to think that they had reached a very nice spot. There was a pile of wood that a woodcutter had left, perfect for building a big strong house.

"Whatever happened to my brother can never happen to me," thought the second little pig. But that night, as the church clock struck twelve, there came a tapping at her door.

"Little pig, little pig, let me come in," a voice said softly. "I'm lonely and hungry. I want a bite to eat."

The little pig's heart gave a thump. Now she knew what had happened to her brother. "Wolf! You don't fool me! You're not coming in, not by the hair on my chinny-chin-chin!" she cried.

"Then I'll huff and I'll puff and I'll blow your house in!" the wolf snarled. "And that'll be the end of you." And it was.

Next morning the third little pig found the wooden house shattered to pieces and all his sister's possessions blowing in the wind. He began to run away but then he thought, "What did my sister and I pass down the road yesterday? A brick factory!" Back he went and bought enough bricks to build a house.

That night the wolf came prowling and tapping again. "I'm a friend of your brother and sister," he called. "Little pig, little pig, let me come in."

"Wolf, you're not coming in here, not by the hair on my chinny-chin-chin!" the third little pig shouted.

"Then I'll huff and I'll puff and I'll blow your house in!" the wolf snarled. He drew a deep breath and huffed and puffed with all his might. A wind that would have torn up whole woods hit the house, but the walls stood firm because they were built of bricks. The wolf huffed and puffed again and again, but only the doors and windows rattled. In a towering rage, the wolf leapt up onto the roof and began to climb down the chimney.

But the third little pig had thought of this. He quickly built a roaring fire in the grate and put a huge pot of water on to boil. Instead of landing in the fireplace, the wolf fell into the pot and was boiled up. His skin popped open and out jumped the little pig's brother and sister! The wolf had gobbled them whole!

How happy the three little pigs were to see each other again! Safe and sound, in the house built of bricks, they lived happily ever after.

Hansel and Gretel

There were once two children called Hansel and Gretel whose mother had died when they were very small. After some years their father, who was a woodcutter, married again. His new wife came from a much better-off family. She hated living in a poor cottage at the edge of the forest and having hardly anything to eat. And she particularly hated her two stepchildren.

One bitter winter evening, when they were in bed, Hansel and Gretel overheard their stepmother say, "We've hardly any food left. If we don't get rid of the children, we'll *all* starve to death."

The father let out a cry. "It's no use arguing," his wife said. "My mind's made up. Tomorrow we'll lose them in the forest."

"Don't worry," Hansel comforted his sister. "We'll find our way home." Later that night he crept outside and filled his pockets with pebbles.

In the morning the family set off. As they walked, Hansel secretly dropped the pebbles one by one behind him to make a trail. At midday the parents lit a fire for the children and promised to be back soon. They disappeared into the forest but, of course, they never returned.

Shivering with fear, while wolves howled all around them, Hansel and Gretel stayed by the fire until the moon came out and lit the trail of pebbles. Quickly they followed it home.

Their father was overjoyed to see them. Their stepmother pretended she was too but her mind hadn't changed. Three days later she decided to try again. That night she locked the door. She wasn't having Hansel collect pebbles this time. But Hansel was clever. When they set off in the morning, he left a trail of crumbs from the crust meant for his dinner.

At midday the parents left the children as before. When they did not return, Hansel and Gretel waited patiently for the moon to light their way home. But this time the trail had gone. Birds had eaten the crumbs!

Now the children really were lost. They wandered through the forest, starving and frightened, for three days and nights. On the third day they caught sight of a snow-white bird in the branches of a tree. The bird sang to them and the children forgot their hunger and ran after it. It led them to an extraordinary house, built with walls of bread, a roof of cake and windows of sparkling sugar.

At once the children forgot their troubles and ran towards the house. Hansel was about to eat a slice of roof and Gretel a piece of window when a voice called from inside, "Who's nibbling my house?" Out of the door came the sweetest-looking old lady. "You poor dears," she said. "Come inside." Soon the children were eating the largest meal they'd had in their lives. That night they slept on feather beds.

But in the morning everything changed. The old lady was a witch who'd built her house of bread and cake to trap unwary children. She dragged Hansel out of bed by his hair and locked him in a shed. Then she pushed Gretel downstairs into the kitchen.

"Your brother's nothing but skin and bone!" she screamed. "Cook for him! Fatten him up! When he's plump enough he'll make me a lovely meal! But eat nothing yourself! It's all for him." Gretel cried and cried but she had to do as the witch said.

Luckily Hansel still had his wits about him. He decided to fool the witch, whose eyesight was not very good. Every morning she came to feel his finger to see if he was fattening up. Instead of his finger, Hansel pushed a chicken bone through the bars of the window for the witch to feel. "No good! Not fat enough!" she shouted. Back into the kitchen she went and forced Gretel to make bigger and bigger meals.

This went on for a month, until at last the witch's patience ran out. "Fat or thin, today I'm baking Hansel pie!" she screamed at Gretel. "Check if the pastry is baking properly." But Gretel had her wits about her too. She knew the witch meant to push her into the oven.

"I can't get my head in! I can't see the pastry!" she wailed. With a blow the witch knocked Gretel aside and pushed her own head into the oven. Gretel summoned all her strength, gave the evil old lady a huge push, and slammed the oven door after her.

Hansel was free, yet the children were still lost. They set off again through the forest. When they reached a river, a duck carried first Hansel and then Gretel across. Suddenly the children recognized where they were. They ran home as fast as they could.

How happy their father was to see them! He cried with joy as he told them that their cruel stepmother had gone back to her family soon after they'd been lost in the forest. He told them how heartbroken he'd been when he realized what he had done.

And there was another surprise in store for him. Hansel emptied out his pockets and Gretel her apron. They were full of gold and diamonds they had found in the witch's house. Now all the family's worries were over and from then on they all lived together in sheer happiness.

The Gingerbread Boy

Once upon a time an old lady thought how nice it would be to have a little boy about the house again.

"A boy?" her husband said. "We're too old for that sort of caper!" But he saw that she'd made up her mind so he said, "Why not bake a gingerbread boy?"

"What a marvellous idea!" the old lady exclaimed. She mixed up the ingredients, rolled out the dough, then cut out the shape of a gingerbread boy.

She gave him currants for eyes, a smiley mouth, a waistcoat and a hat. She even put buttons down the front of his waistcoat and go faster stripes on his shoes! Then she popped him into the oven to bake.

When the timer on the cooker rang, the old lady opened the oven door. But the gingerbread boy didn't lie still on the baking tray. He leapt straight out onto the floor and ran away through the kitchen door. The astonished old man and lady called to him to come back, but the gingerbread boy felt very grown-up and he shouted,

"Run, run, as fast as you can,
You won't catch me, I'm the gingerbread man!"

Down the road he ran, through a stile and into a field where a cow was chewing grass.

"Hey!" the cow mooed. "Stop and give me a bite to eat!"

The gingerbread boy thought that was really funny. "I've run away from a man and a woman, and now I'll run away from you!" Putting on speed, he shouted,

> "Run, run, as fast as you can,
> You won't catch me, I'm the gingerbread man!"

The cow ran after him in a rather wobbly sort of way, but it was no use. She couldn't catch him.

Next the gingerbread boy came to a horse. "Hey!" the horse neighed. "I'm hungry. Give me a nibble!"

But the gingerbread boy just laughed. "I've run away from a man and a woman and a cow, and now I'll run away from you!" He ran even faster, shouting,

> "Run, run, as fast as you can,
> You won't catch me, I'm the gingerbread man!"

The horse galloped after him but he couldn't catch him.

Next the gingerbread boy met some joggers panting along a path. "Hey! Stop!" they called. "We haven't had our breakfast yet!"

But the gingerbread boy just skipped past them. "I've run away from a man and a woman and a cow and a horse, and now I'll run away from you!" Running even faster, he shouted,

"Run, run, as fast as you can,
You won't catch me, I'm the gingerbread man!"

The joggers ran as fast as they could after him, but there was no way they were ever going to catch him.

Then the gingerbread boy came to a river and there he had to stop. He could run but he couldn't swim.

There was a fox in the hedge who'd seen all that had gone on. He came strolling out. "Don't worry, sweet little gingerbread boy," he said. "I wouldn't dream of eating you. I've already eaten a hen and a turkey and some leftovers from a dustbin this morning. Do you want to cross the river?"

"Of course I do," the gingerbread boy said, looking over his shoulder at the man and the woman and the cow and the horse and the joggers, who were getting closer and closer.

"Then hop onto my tail," the fox said. "I'll swim you across." The gingerbread boy hopped onto the fox's tail and off they set, leaving all the gingerbread boy's pursuers behind.

When they'd gone a little way across the river, the fox said, "My tail's sinking into the water. You don't want to get wet, do you? Climb onto my back." The gingerbread boy did so.

They'd gone a little further when the fox said, "Now my body's beginning to sink too. Climb onto the tip of my nose. You'll be safer there. Gingerbread and water don't mix, do they?" The gingerbread boy climbed onto the tip of the fox's nose.

The moment the fox reached the other side of the river, he flipped the gingerbread boy up into the air and down into his mouth.

Snap! A quarter of him had gone.

Snap! A half of him had gone.

Snap! The fox ate the rest of him all in one go.

And that was the end of the gingerbread boy who'd been too fast for the man and the woman and the cow and the horse and the joggers, but not quick enough for the fox!

25

Little Red Riding Hood

Granny lived not far away, but to get to her cottage you had to walk through Bunny's Wood (though no one had seen a rabbit there for ages—you'll see why in a moment).

"Little Red Riding Hood!" her mother called. "Granny's still not very well. Put on your cloak and the pretty red riding hood she made for your birthday. Then pop over with this custard tart and pot of butter I've got ready for her tea."

So Little Red Riding Hood slipped on her cloak, fastened her riding hood under her chin, and set off.

"Remember to keep to the path in Bunny's Wood!" her mother called after her.

"Of course, Mummy," Little Red Riding Hood called back. "I always do."

She was only a little way inside the wood when there was a noise in the bushes and out onto the path jumped a great big wolf. Little Red Riding Hood nearly dropped her basket in fright, but actually the wolf seemed quite friendly. "Where are you off to, little girl?" he asked.

"To my granny's," Little Red Riding Hood replied. "It's the first cottage you come to at the end of Bunny's Wood. Granny's not very well. And my name's not 'little girl', it's Little Red Riding Hood."

"Sorry," said the wolf. "I didn't know. Tell you what—why don't I run ahead and tell Granny you're on your way? And, Little Red Riding Hood, don't stray off the path, will you? We don't want anything to happen to you before you get to Granny's, do we?"

Off skipped the wolf—just in time! For around the corner was a woodcutter. The wolf hadn't eaten Little Red Riding Hood there and then because he knew there was a woodcutter nearby who might come to her rescue.

While Little Red Riding Hood made her way along the path, stopping every couple of minutes to pick flowers or chase butterflies or listen to the birds singing, the wolf took a short cut. He knocked at Granny's door.

"Who is it?" the little old lady called.

The wolf disguised his voice. "It's me, Little Red Riding Hood. I've brought some good things for tea."

"The door's on the latch, my darling," Granny called. And in went the wolf. How hungry he was! He hadn't eaten for days. He swallowed Granny whole, from her head to her feet.

About ten minutes later, Little Red Riding Hood knocked on Granny's door.

"Who is it?" the wolf called softly.

"It's me, Little Red Riding Hood."

"The door's on the latch, my darling," the wolf called. "Come on in."

For a moment Little Red Riding Hood hesitated. Wasn't there something funny about Granny's voice? Then she remembered that Granny had a cold. She lifted the latch and in she went.

The wolf was lying in bed wearing the little old lady's nightie and nightcap and glasses. The sheet was pulled right up over his face and he'd drawn the curtains to make it nice and dark.

"Put the things down there," he said, "then snuggle up to me, my darling."

Little Red Riding Hood put the custard tart and butter down on the bedside table but she didn't get onto the bed right away. Something suddenly struck her.

"What great big hairy arms you have, Granny!"

"All the better to hug you with, my darling!" the wolf said.

"And what great big ears you have, Granny!"

"All the better to hear you with, my darling!" the wolf said.

"And what great big eyes you have, Granny!"

"All the better to see you with, my darling!" the wolf said.

"And what great big teeth you have, Granny!"

"All the better to eat you with, my darling!"

With that the wolf was so excited he couldn't contain himself any longer. He threw the bedclothes aside, jumped out of bed and swallowed Little Red Riding Hood whole, head first. Then he felt so happy and full of people that he lay back and went to sleep.

Unfortunately for the wolf, he was a loud snorer. A passing huntsman heard the snores. Thinking something was wrong with Granny, he crept into the cottage. He saw at once what had happened.

"I've been looking for you for months, you wicked creature," he cried, and he hit the wolf on the head with his axe handle. Then very carefully he slit the wolf's tummy open. Out popped Little Red Riding Hood and out popped Granny! They were completely unharmed.

Granny saw the custard tart and butter she'd been brought for her tea and, well, wolfed it down. Little Red Riding Hood promised Granny that she'd never be tricked by a wolf again. As she skipped home, she noticed that the rabbits had come out of hiding and Bunny's Wood was full of bunnies again.

"What a funny afternoon it's been," she thought.

Jack and the Beanstalk

There was once a poor widow. Her son Jack was a lazy boy, so they had very little money. One sad day things got so bad that the widow decided to sell the only thing they had left. She sent Jack off to market with Milky White, their cow, telling him to get the best price he could.

Jack was only part way along the road when he bumped into a funny old man. The old man eyed the cow and said, "My boy, I'll swap her for something very precious." He pulled five beans out of his pocket.

"Beans?" Jack said doubtfully.

"They're magic ones," the old man explained. That made Jack's mind up. He handed over Milky White and went home very satisfied with his bargain.

"Mum! Look what I've got!" he shouted. Jack's mother wasn't so happy, though. She threw the beans out of the window and a saucepan at Jack! Then she sent him to bed without any supper.

In the morning, however, Jack could hardly believe his eyes. Something was growing outside his bedroom window. He poked his head out. It wasn't a tree or a giant sunflower but a beanstalk that grew straight up into the sky. At once Jack clambered out of his window and began to climb the beanstalk.

Half an hour later he found himself in another country where everything was much larger. Across the fields was a very big house. A woman answered the door.

"What about a bite to eat?" Jack asked cheekily.

"All right," the woman said, "but if my husband the ogre comes, you'll have to make yourself scarce. He eats children."

Jack decided to take the chance, but he'd hardly sat down on the table when there was a roar outside.

"Fee-fi-fo-fum,
  I smell the blood of an Englishman.
  Be he alive or be he dead,
  I'll grind his bones to make my bread."

"Quick! In the oven!" the woman said to Jack. "Nonsense, sweetheart, you can smell the scraps of yesterday's child I gave the cat," she shouted to her husband.

After his meal the ogre began counting bags of gold. That soon put him to sleep. Out sneaked Jack and stole a bag. He threw it down the beanstalk and scampered after. His mother could hardly believe their good luck.

But a few months later, all the gold spent, Jack decided to go back to the other land. Up the beanstalk he climbed. This time, however, the ogre's wife was more suspicious.

"Last time you came, a bag of gold went missing," she complained. "The fuss that caused!" All the same she let Jack in.

Very soon the ogre came along. *"Fee-fi-fo-fum,"* he started to roar. Jack hid in the oven again.

"Nonsense, angel," the ogre's wife said. "It's only the smell of that baby broth you had yesterday. Eat your buffalo pie."

After he'd eaten, the ogre shouted, "Wife, bring me my hen." His wife brought it. "Lay!" the ogre commanded, and to Jack's amazement the hen laid a golden egg. Naturally Jack stole the hen too.

By now Jack and his mother were well off, but after a year Jack decided to try his luck again. Up he climbed. This time he sneaked his way past the ogre's wife and hid in her copper pan.

In came the ogre. *"Fee-fi-fo-fum,"* he started.

"If it's that dratted boy again, he'll be in the oven, dearest," his wife said.

But of course Jack wasn't.

"I know he's here somewhere," the ogre rumbled, but although they searched high and low they couldn't find him.

This time after his meal the ogre got out a golden harp. "Sing!" he commanded, and the harp lullabyed him to sleep. Now Jack wanted that harp more than anything he'd ever wanted before. He climbed onto the snoring giant's knee, jumped onto the table and grabbed it.

"Master!" the harp cried. Jack jumped off the table. The ogre galloped after them. "Master!" the harp cried again, when Jack was halfway down the beanstalk. The ogre began to climb down after him.

"Mum!" Jack called. "Mum! An axe! Quick! Quick!" Together they chopped at the beanstalk and down it tumbled, ogre and all. He died instantly.

"Phew!" Jack said. "That was a close one!"

After that Jack and his mother lived rich people's lives. The hen laid golden eggs whenever they told it to. People paid to hear the golden harp play. It's even said that Jack married a beautiful princess. Maybe he did!

Goldilocks and the Three Bears

Once upon a time three bears lived in a house in the woods. They were called Tiny Little Bear, Middle-sized Bear and Great Big Bear. Their house, which they kept very spick and span, was full of just the right-sized things – bowls, cups, spoons, chairs, beds – anything you could think of.

One morning it was Great Big Bear's turn to get breakfast. He ladled the porridge into the bowls, just the right amount in each. But when they sat down to eat, the porridge was far too hot. The three bears decided to go for a walk while it cooled.

Two minutes after they had set off, who should come past their house but a little girl called Goldilocks. Goldilocks was a naughty spoiled brat who always did exactly what she wanted. She shouldn't even have been in the woods (her mummy had sent her to the shop to buy some milk). But there she was and she knew the bears were out walking. She tried the door. It wasn't locked, so in she went.

Goldilocks spied what was on the table. "Porridge!" She licked her lips. "My favourite!" She tried the porridge in Great Big Bear's bowl first. "Ugh!" she said. "That's far too hot." She spat it out.

Next she tried Middle-sized Bear's bowl. "Ugh! That's far too cold!" She spat that out too.

Last she tried Tiny Little Bear's. "Goody!" she said. "That's just right!" She gobbled it up. "Bother!" she said. (Actually she said a far worse word.) "There wasn't much in there."

Then, because she needed a rest after all her wandering about in the woods, Goldilocks tried Great Big Bear's chair. "Hard as rocks," she said. "No good to me."

Next she sat in Middle-sized Bear's. "Miles too soft," she said.

Last she tried Tiny Little Bear's chair. "Just right," she said. At least she thought it was until her bottom went through the seat and the chair collapsed! Again she used a very bad word.

But Goldilocks was determined to get a rest. Upstairs she went and opened the bedroom door. First she tried Great Big Bear's bed, but that left her head too much in the air.

Next she tried Middle-sized Bear's. That left her feet too far up.

Last she tried Tiny Little Bear's. It was perfect! Without even taking off her shoes, she tucked herself in and went straight to sleep, dreaming of all the naughty things she'd get up to when she was older.

Meanwhile the bears returned home. They hung their coats up neatly and went to eat their porridge. Except, except…

"Who's been at my porridge?" Great Big Bear growled. "They've even left the spoon in it."

"And who's been at mine," asked Middle-sized Bear, "and done the same?"

"And who's been at mine, and eaten it all up?" Tiny Little Bear sobbed.

The three bears looked about. Someone had been in their house without permission and they didn't like that one bit.

"Somebody's been sitting in my chair," Great Big Bear growled, "and tossed my cushion on the floor!"

"Somebody's been sitting in my chair too," growled Middle-sized Bear. "My cushion's squashed."

"And somebody's been sitting in my chair and broken it," Tiny Little Bear said. He began to cry again.

"Sshh!" Great Big Bear said. "What's that noise?" The three bears listened.

"It's someone snoring," said Middle-sized Bear. The three bears looked at each other.

"They're still here!" Tiny Little Bear said. Upstairs they crept.

They went into the bedroom. "Somebody's been lying on my bed," Great Big Bear growled. "My cover's all creased."

"Somebody's been lying on my bed too," Middle-sized Bear grumbled. "The pillow's all out of place."

"And somebody's been lying *in* my bed, and they're *still* lying in it," squeaked Tiny Little Bear.

Great Big Bear's voice hadn't woken Goldilocks—she'd thought it was the wind roaring in her dream. Middle-sized Bear's voice hadn't woken her either—she'd thought it was her teacher shouting and that didn't frighten her at all. But Tiny Little Bear's shrill voice woke her straightaway.

She took one look at the bears standing in a row along one side of the bed, jumped out the other side and dived through the window. She landed in a bed of flowers only planted last week, knocked over the bird-table and ran straight out of the garden.

"She hasn't shut the gate," Middle-sized Bear complained with a sigh. "One of us will have to do it."

And what happened to Goldilocks no one knows. Maybe her mother just scolded her for not bringing the milk. Or maybe she did something worse, when she found out what Goldilocks had *really* been up to!

The Ugly Duckling

Deep in the bushes a duck was sitting on her eggs. She was bored with being on her own, so when the eggs began to crack she jumped off the nest with a quack of pleasure.

"Now I can get back to the farmyard," she thought, "and show off my new family!" She counted her cheeping ducklings to make sure they were all there. Oh no! One egg hadn't hatched.

"That's a large one left in your nest," another duck who was passing said. "I bet it's a turkey's."

"A turkey's egg? No, it's mine," the mother duck said crossly. With a sigh she settled back on top of it.

When the last duckling hatched, it was very large and ugly. To tell the truth the mother duck was rather ashamed of it.

All the same, her other ducklings were as pretty as could be and she didn't want to stay away from the farmyard another minute. She led her little family straight out onto the water.

"At least the ugly one swims very well," she said to herself. "So it can't be a turkey. Turkeys can't swim, can they? Perhaps it will get prettier as it grows older. Perhaps it will stop being so big."

Unfortunately the opposite happened. The ugly duckling grew bigger every day and all the other ducks noticed how different he was. Hardly a minute passed without him being attacked and bitten and jeered at. Even his brothers and sisters quacked, "We wish the cat would get you!" The chickens bullied him and the girl who fed them kicked him out of the way.

Finally the ugly duckling couldn't bear it any longer. He flew over the fence and scuttled away until he came to the place where the wild ducks lived. But the wild ducks thought he was ugly too and would have nothing to do with him.

So the duckling became the loneliest creature in the world. Even the little birds from the trees and hedges flew away when he came near. "It's because I'm so ugly," he said to himself.

He wandered here and there, always on his own. Once he made good friends with two young wild geese, but they flew away to escape the hunters. Once an old lady took him into her house, but her pets, a hen and a tom cat, laughed at the strange bird for liking the water and not being able to lay eggs. So the ugly duckling ran away again.

The leaves turned yellow and brown. Snow-laden clouds hung over the land. One evening at sunset, a flock of tall, handsome birds with dazzling white feathers came out of the bushes in front of the duckling. They had long, elegant necks that swayed backwards and forwards.

"Wait!" called the duckling, but the birds spread their enormous wings and were soon high in the sky. The duckling couldn't help himself. He turned round and round in the water like a spinning top and dived to the bottom in sheer excitement. From his throat came a strange loud cry, so strange it frightened him. He couldn't forget those white-feathered birds. Whatever they were, he loved them.

It was a long, hard winter. Several times the ugly duckling nearly died. Once he became frozen in the ice and a passing farmer had to rescue him. But at last spring came and the duckling found that he could fly properly, not just flip-flapping above the water but soaring high in the sky.

One day he was testing his new-found strength when, below in a river, he saw more of the beautiful white birds. He did not hesitate. "I'll fly down," he thought. "Even if I'm ugly, I want to be near them." And he landed on the water.

Two children were throwing bread to the white birds from the river bank. When they saw the duckling, they called to their mother, "Look! A new swan! He's even more beautiful than the others!"

At first the duckling didn't realize what they meant. Instead he bowed his head in shame as the tall white birds turned to look at him. "Kill me!" he thought. "I don't care what you do."

Then, as he raised his head, he caught sight of his own reflection in the water. And he couldn't believe what he saw. His neck was long. He had beautiful white feathers.

"Welcome!" the other swans called. They glided towards him, not angry with him or full of hate like the birds in the farmyard, but bowing their necks gracefully towards him as if to say, "You're beautiful!"

"A swan!" he said in wonder. "I'm not an ugly duckling at all. I'm a swan!"

The Elves and the Shoemaker

There was once a shoemaker who was very poor although he was a master craftsman. Every day he seemed to get even poorer. In the end he sold so few shoes that he had no money to buy leather to make new ones. At last he only had one piece of leather left.

That night he cut out the leather and, with a sigh, left it on his workbench ready to stitch up into his last pair of shoes in the morning. As he went upstairs to bed, he could only think that if a miracle didn't happen he would have to sell his shop.

The next morning, when he opened his workroom door, the shoemaker saw something extraordinary. On his bench stood the most beautifully made pair of shoes he'd ever seen. He darted to pick them up. He turned them round in his hands. He couldn't have made them better himself!

That morning a rich man walked past the shop. He saw the pair of shoes in the window and liked them so much that he was willing to pay twice what the shoemaker asked!

Now the shoemaker had enough money to buy leather for two more pairs of shoes. That evening he cut them out and left them on his workbench. In the morning, to his great joy, the leather had been stitched up into *two* beautiful pairs of shoes. The shoemaker was able to sell them for enough money to buy leather for *four* pairs of shoes.

For some time, things went on like this. Soon the shoemaker's little shop became so famous that rich ladies and gentlemen from all over the country came to see what he had to sell.

But one day towards Christmas, the shoemaker, who was a kind-hearted man, said to his wife, "Don't you think we ought to see who's doing us this favour? Think how poor we once were and how well off we are now. Tonight let's stay downstairs with the light off and see who comes." So instead of going to bed, the shoemaker and his wife hid behind the workroom door. As quiet as mice they waited.

As midnight struck from the tower of the parish church, the shoemaker's wife nudged her husband. Two tiny elves, dressed in rags, were clambering up onto the workbench. They ran around looking at what work they had to do. Then they seized the shoemaker's tools and began. As they worked they sang,

> "Stitch the, stitch the, stitch the shoes,
>   Fit for kings and queens to choose!
>   Dart the needle, pull the stitch.
>   Work, work, work, to make the cobbler rich!"

Long before dawn they'd finished their work and slipped away.

The shoemaker and his wife got up late next morning. Over breakfast the wife said, "Think how cold those poor little creatures must have been! Their feet were bare and their clothes were just rags. It made me shiver just to look at them. Don't you think we ought to make them a present to say 'thank you' for all the work they've done for us?"

The shoemaker agreed, and he and his wife set to work immediately. That night they left the tiniest clothes and shoes you could imagine on the workbench.

At midnight, as the church clock struck, the elves appeared again. At first they seemed puzzled to find no shoes to stitch, but suddenly they realized what kind of presents had been left for them. With whoops of joy they pulled on the tiny clothes and shoes. Then they began to dance all around the room, leaping on and off the table, balancing along the backs of the chairs, and swinging off the curtains. As they played they sang,

"The shoemaker has no more need of elves.
Now let him stock his own shelves!"

With that they ran out of the door and across the churchyard. They never came back. The shoemaker was sad to see them go but he could hardly complain after all the work they'd done for him. And they seemed to leave a little of their magic behind them, for he and his wife were lucky for the rest of their lives.

45